Usborne

Little Children's Cut, Stick and Tear Book

Illustrated by Katie Turner

Designed by Josephine Thompson
Words by Matthew Oldham

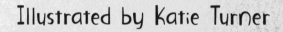

You'll find paper to cut and tear at the back of this book.

Notes for grown-ups

The activities in this book give little children a chance to work on their scissor skills and to make shapes by tearing.

To use this book you'll need a pair of round-ended scissors for careful cutting and some glue to stick the paper to the page. For some activities you can tear the paper, without scissors.

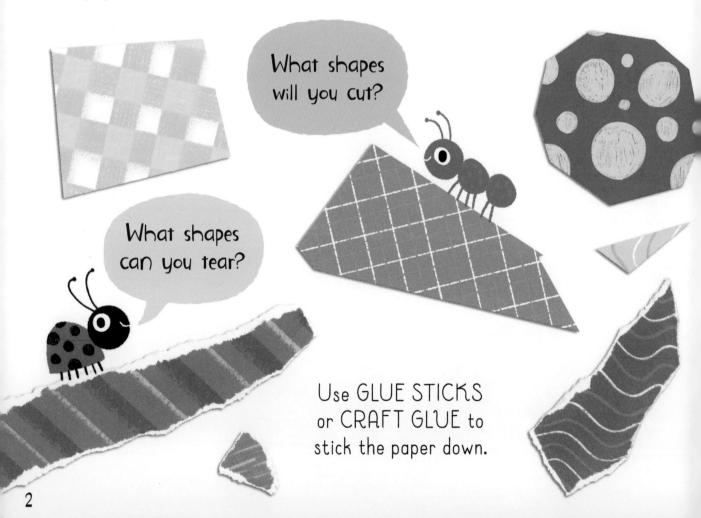

What shapes will you cut?

What shapes can you tear?

Use GLUE STICKS or CRAFT GLUE to stick the paper down.

The THICK paper at the back of this book is best for cutting.
The THIN paper is best for tearing. You can also use your own paper to do more sticking - from scraps of wrapping paper to old newspapers or magazines.

For some activities, there are shapes for you to cut around, like this.

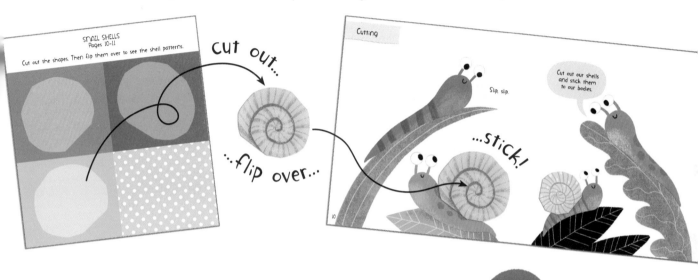

cut out...

...flip over...

...stick!

SNAIL SHELLS
Pages 10-11
Cut out the shapes. Then flip them over to see the shell patterns.

Cutting

Slip, slip.

Cut out our shells and stick them to our bodies.

10

For other activities, you can try snipping into the paper, like this.

Snip into the paper, but not all the way.

There are all kinds of ways children can use this book. They don't need to be neat, or worry about sticking paper in the "wrong" place. Let them experiment, and, most of all, have fun.

3

Cutting

Cut out shapes to stick on our shells.

4

5

Please cut some more spiky shapes to stick on Dino's back.

Please cut out tail shapes to stick to our bodies.

Snip along the edge to give our tails some extra SWISH.

9

Slip, slip.

10

11

It's sleepy time! Cut out blankets to cover the beds.

Make tassels by snipping into the blankets' edges.

Cutting

This tall flower needs some petals.

Flutter, flutter!
Cut some shapes
to decorate
my wings.

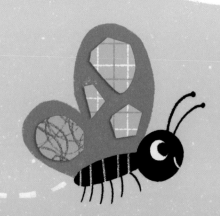

16

Cut some stripes and stick them onto Tiger.

19

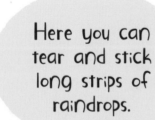

Here you can tear and stick long strips of raindrops.

Tearing

23

Tear shapes and stick them on my head and give me a tail.

This bird needs some fancy feathers.

28

Tear some big, bushy tails to stick on our bodies, please.

Stick some leaf shapes on these branches, too.

31

Tearing

Boo! Tear up eight spindly legs to stick on me.

First published in 2022 by Usborne Publishing Limited, 83-85 Saffron Hill, London EC1N 8RT, United Kingdom. usborne.com

FISH TAILS
Pages 8-9

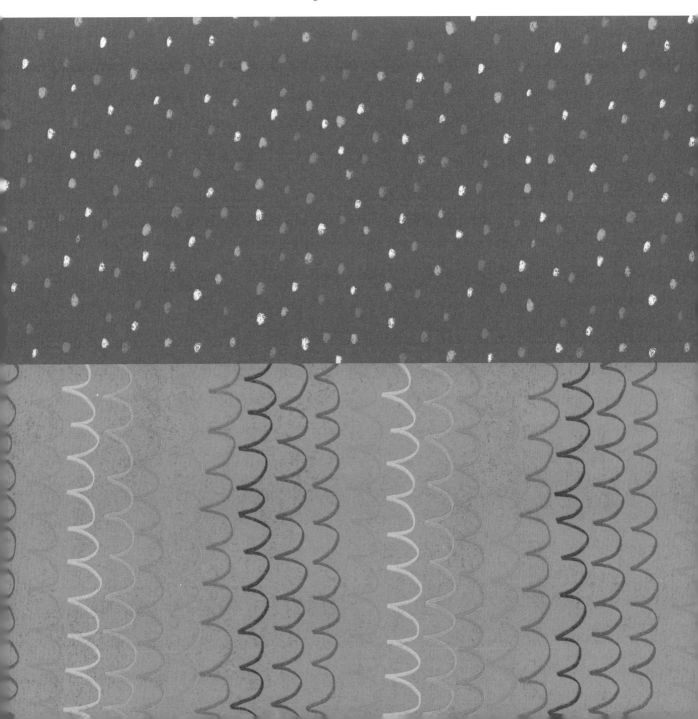

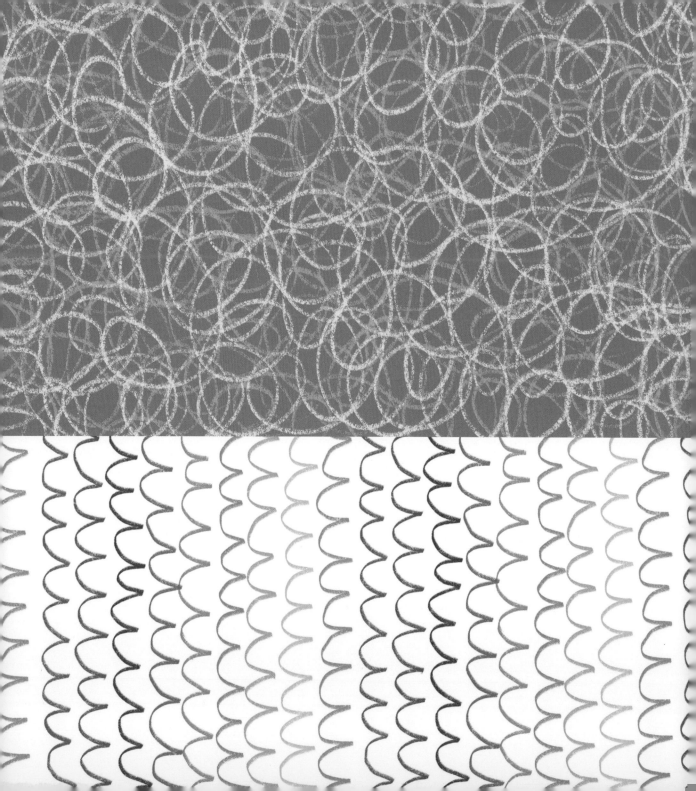

SNAIL SHELLS
Pages 10-11

Cut out the shapes. Then flip them over to see the shell patterns.

FLOWERS
Pages 14-15

Cut out these shapes and flip them over
to see the flowers you have made.

You can snip along the
edge of this flower...

...and all around the outside of this one.

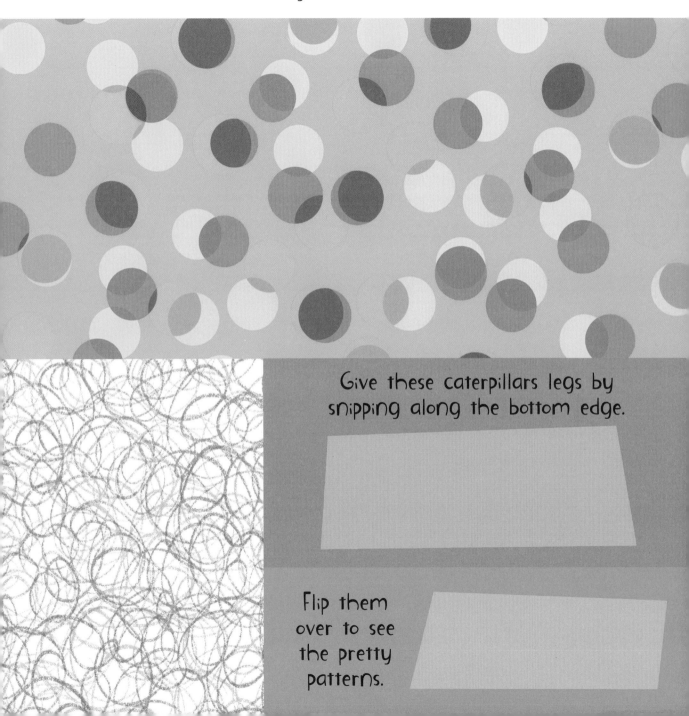

Give these caterpillars legs by snipping along the bottom edge.

Flip them over to see the pretty patterns.

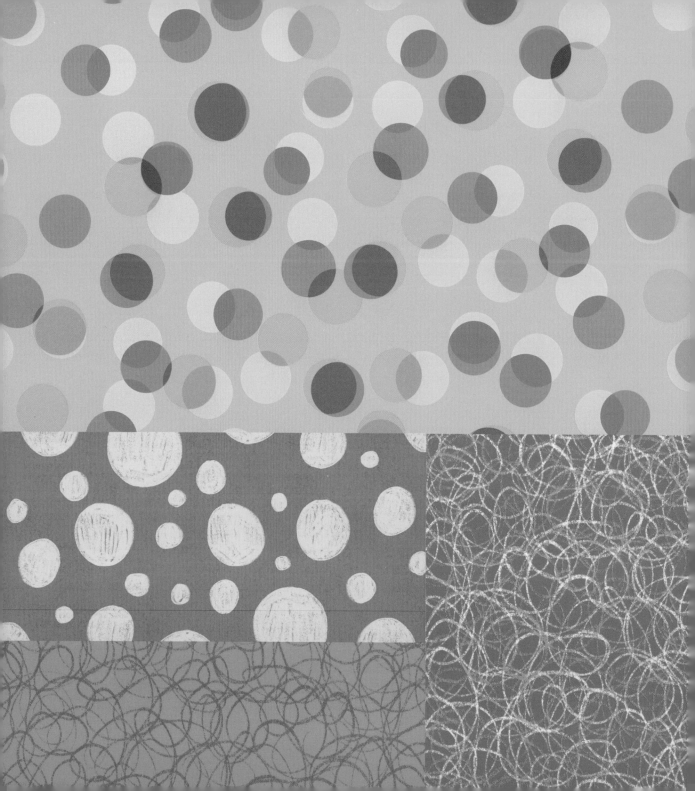

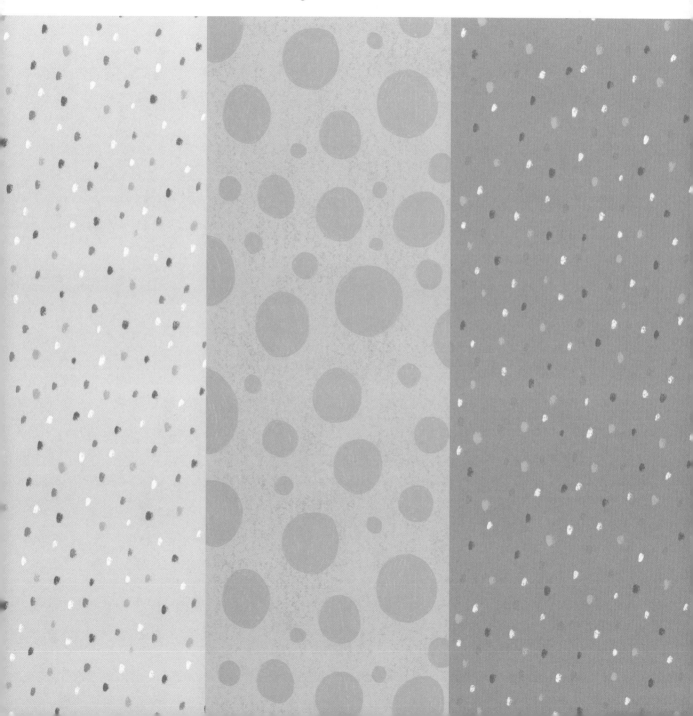

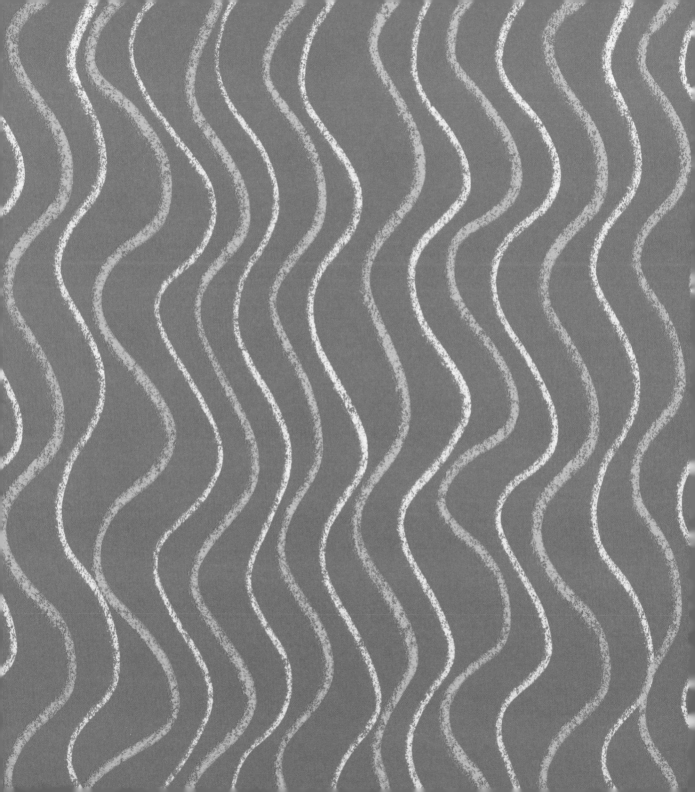

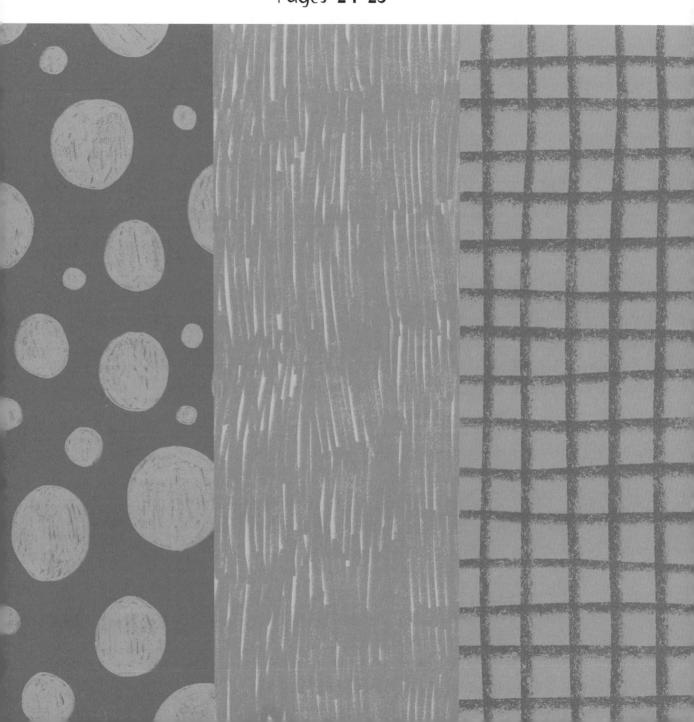

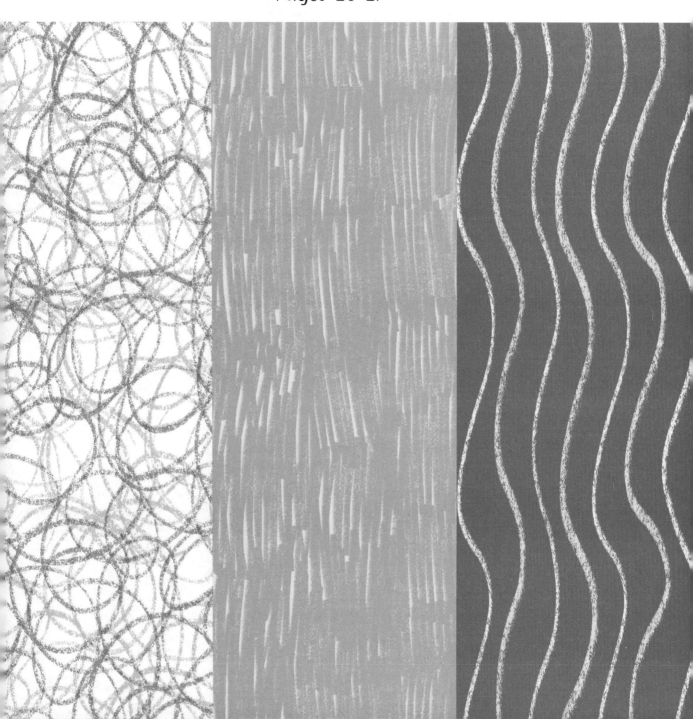

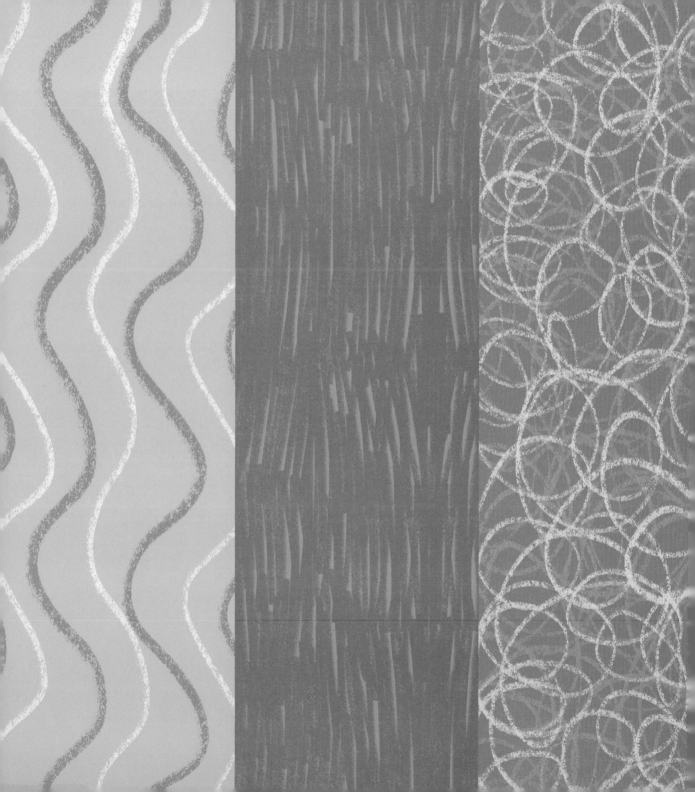

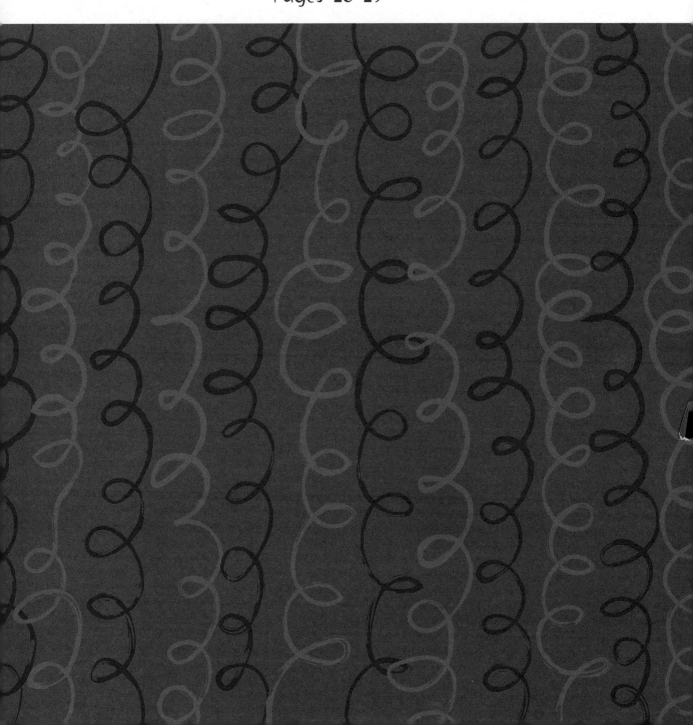